Wildlife
in
Morgan's Land

Cover photographs
Lesser horseshoe bat *Rhinolophus hipposideros*. Merthyr Mawr, 1972.

Wildlife in Morgan's Land

*A tribute to the late Arthur Morgan
photographer and naturalist
of Porthcawl, Mid Glamorgan*

1980
THE GLAMORGAN NATURALISTS' TRUST

First published in October, 1980

© The Glamorgan Naturalists' Trust
147, St. Helens Road, Swansea, West Glamorgan.

ISBN 0 905928 12 1

Designed and printed in Wales by
D. Brown & Sons Ltd., Bridgend and Cowbridge, Glamorgan.

Foreword

That a book should be produced of some of his works, and in his memory, would certainly have surprised Arthur Morgan; the production and the surprise together reflect a man who was much loved and whose exceptional qualities were obvious to everyone who had anything to do with him—but who was himself too modest (and too busy!) to bother with the bubble reputation.

By trade, and for most of his life, he was a plumber (and, as I have personal reason to know, a very good one!). By inclination he was a naturalist and a photographer, and for the last two of his short span of forty-one years, these activities and his job happily coincided in his work at the Kenfig Local Nature Reserve. In both spheres he was entirely self-taught, and in both he reached the very highest standards; as a naturalist he was rightly described as "unquestionably the most skilled and dedicated" in the three Glamorgan counties; as a photographer . . . let the following pages speak for him.

It was a privilege to know him; it is a privilege to write this brief foreword to what is essentially his book.

MURRAY McLAGGAN
Merthyr Mawr House
April, 1980

Introduction to the photographs

The black-and-white photographs in this book include several that were chosen by Arthur for exhibitions furthering the cause of conservation in the Glamorgan counties. Many were submitted by him for critical comment by fellow-members of the Nature Photographic Society, and some won recognition and awards at the Welsh Photographic Federation's annual salons.

Also included are prints which Arthur doubtlessly never intended for publication, but which, in reflecting his early enthusiasm and growing skills, are bound to inspire and please.

Where information is available in Arthur's notes, a brief description of the subject and site is given in the captions to the photographs. In places I have used my own, all too limited knowledge of Arthur's history to place the work in context.

I am indebted to Arthur's sister, Mrs. Mair Jones, and to her family, for making available to the Glamorgan Naturalists' Trust this very special material. This book could never have been produced without their help, nor without the hard work of Hugh and Audrey Phillips on behalf of the Glamorgan Naturalists' Trust committees, nor without the many contributions of advice and financial support from so many friends and local naturalists.

I am sure that this production will stimulate interest in the colour photographs of Arthur's which form such a large part of the exhibition at the Kenfig Reserve Centre, but more especially, I hope that it gives the reader an insight into Arthur's "field-craft" and his love of natural things.

STEVE MOON
Kenfig Local Nature Reserve
Mid Glamorgan
June, 1980

1   (opposite) Skylark *Alauda arvensis* photographed at Nottage, June 1969.
    Arthur's comments: "This nest was cut into when the hayfield was being cut. The tractor driver saw the bird come off the nest and left a small piece uncut. We covered the nest with branches from the hedge."

2 *(opposite)* In order to minimise disturbance to the birds he photographed Arthur invariably used some form of hide. This tower-hide, in a quarry at Tythegston, had to be built in stages in order to get the subject (a kestrel *Falco tinnunculus*) used to its presence.

3 Kestrel *Falco tinnunculus*. (Tythegston quarry).

4 Male house sparrow *Passer domesticus*. So common a bird is often overlooked as a subject for photography. The Royal Photographic Society of Great Britain accepted and exhibited this photograph at the International Exhibition in London, 1968.

5   Female house sparrow *Passer domesticus*, feeding young.

6   Dunnock *Prunella modularis*. Merthyr Mawr, 1969.

7   Blue tit *Parus caeruleus*, feeding young. Nottage, May 1969.

8 Wren. *Troglodytes troglodytes*. This nest was in the same cottage as the swallow nest opposite. Arthur often joked that the eight-inch nail was there for reinforcement! Merthyr Mawr, July 1972.

9   Swallow *Hirundo rustica*. Nest site was in a thatched cottage which was being renovated. Two broods of swallow were successfully reared. The second brood were not flying until late September. Merthyr Mawr, July 1972.

10   Mistle thrush *Turdus viscivorus*. Merthyr Mawr, June 1968.

11   A thrush, recently fledged.

12   Wren *Troglodytes troglodytes*. A hedgerow in Nottage, July 1967.

13 Tree-creeper *Certhia familiaris*, well-camouflaged at its nest site in Merthyr Mawr
park, May 1967.

14   Spotted Flycatcher *Muscicapa striata*. Merthyr Mawr, July 1969.

15 Robin *Erithacus rubecula*, photographed at Ewenny, 1972.

16,17,18 A series of remarkable photographs. The meadow pipit *Anthus pratensis* on this page is coping with the ever-increasing demands of a growing cuckoo *Cuculus canorus*. *Opposite top* is an unusual photograph of territorial aggression between rival meadow pipits *Anthus pratensis*, and below is an opportunistic shot of a skylark *Alauda arvensis* removing a faecal sac from its nest.

19   Redstart *Phoenicurus phoenicurus*. This is the sombre-plumaged female of a pair that Arthur photographed at Hafod, on the fringe of Margam forest, June 1972.

20 Redstart *Phoenicurus phoenicurus*. The male of the Hafod pair.

21 This migrant whinchat *Saxicola rubetra*, was photographed at Sker, September 1968.

22 A male wheatear *Oenanthe oenanthe*. Bardsey Island, September 1970.

23   Rock pipit *Anthus spinoletta*. Photographed at its nest at Sker Rocks.

24   Wheatear *Oenanthe oenanthe*. A female or juvenile, on the beach at Bardsey, September 1970.

(*opposite*) Herring gull *Larus argentatus*. Nest sites are often on precarious cliff ledges.

27   Pied wagtail *Motacilla alba*. This photograph was taken in June 1974 at Hafod, Margam.

26   (*opposite*)   The peace and tranquillity of family life! Mute swans *Cygnus olor* at the pool in Newton, near Porthcawl.

28   Grey phalarope *Phalaropus fulicarius*, on Sker pool, 1974. Strong westerly winds during September resulted in the appearance of six of these unusual waders in the Kenfig/Sker area.

29   Manx Shearwater *Puffinus puffinus*, photographed on Skomer Island, 1974.

30 Chough *Pyrrhocorax pyrrhocorax*, on the beach at Bardsey Island, September 1970.

31 Arthur had noticed that two pairs of choughs regularly visited the beach at Bardsey Island and dug into the sand for invertebrates. The birds appeared to have favourite digging-places, and this photograph was obtained from a hide close to one of these sites where the holes had been thoughtfully topped-up with maggots!

32 (*opposite*) Little owl *Athene noctua*, bringing a short-tailed field vole *Microtus agrestis* to a nest in Porthcawl, June 1967.

33 On this occasion the food item brought to the nest by the little owl was a moth.

34   A juvenile barn owl *Tyto alba*. Arthur had a strong interest in photographing owls and was fortunate enough to be given permission to take photographs at the nest.

35 A well-grown juvenile tawny owl *Strix aluco*.

36   Not all of Arthur's subjects were warm-blooded. This viviparous lizard *Lacerta vivipara*, was photographed on Skomer Island.

37   Slow worm *Anguis fragilis*, on Skomer Island.

38 The common frog *Rana temporaria*.

39 (*opposite*) This bank vole *Clethrionomys glareolus* was photographed at bait—a mixture of oatmeal, peanut butter, raisins, suet, paraffin-wax and a 'scent-additive'. Porthcawl, April 1972.

41 Woodmouse *Apodemus sylvaticus*, Skomer Island, 1974. For these photographs an electronic-flash was used. Arthur was mammal-recorder for the counties of Glamorgan, but he never missed an opportunity to study them in other parts of the country.

40 (*opposite*) Common shrew *Sorex araneus*, warily stretching towards bait. Porthcawl, 1972.

42 Always ready to overcome a photographic challenge when it came to recording the animals he loved, Arthur had perfected the technique of photographing bats. This is a Lesser horseshoe bat *Rhinolophus hipposideros* captured on film leaving its roost-site at Merthyr Mawr, 1972.